Open minds:
anything is possible!

Author: Rebecca Wilson Macsovits
Creative: Milena Kirkova

Library of Congress # 2 0 1 9 9 2 0 3 5 9

The **YOU** Series
Harking, LLC
Englewood, CO 80113

www.guionthelion.com

Author : Macsovits, Rebecca
ISBN : 978-1-7923-2767-4

G., H., and R.—
Seeing the world through your
eyes has only enriched mine.
Thank you for being you!

Guion
THE LION

BY
REBECCA
WILSON
MACSOVITS

"Rae! Wake up!
You have to see this!"
exclaimed Guion the Lion.

Under her breath,
Rae the Bushbaby
mumbled, "I cannot
think of ONE reason
to be excited right now."

"Ta Da!" Guion squinted his eyes, tilted his head, and swept his arms out wide.

"The kingdom is preparing for battle against the fierce dragon. I couldn't let my best friend miss the epic occasion!"

"Seriously, Guion? You woke me up for this?" cried Rae. "An ugly, brown dirt mound that I can't see around. Oh, great! I see the termites are hard at work making this monstrosity even bigger!"

"And that scary 'dragon' is just Wilson the Giraffe chewing with her mouth open. I think you need to get your eyes checked."

Guion looked back at the castle and thought for a minute. Smiling, he said, "I know exactly what to show you, Rae! Let's go!"

Wilson had overheard her friends and stopped to take a look. She squinted her eyes, tilted her head, and then she heard the knight say, "Hello, Giraffe. Do you seek passage over our kingdom?"

Determined to share his fun, Guion
guided Rae to the watering hole. With the
help of a long reed and a tilt of his head,
Guion looked at the underwater landscape.

"We've just discovered _Queen Anne's Revenge_
commanded by Captain Blackbeard.
Oh, look! We aren't the first—the mermaids
are playing hide-and-seek in the ship."

Eager to see the pirate ship herself, Rae grabbed the reed. After a moment, Rae lifted her head and groaned.

"What are you talking about? There's no ship! It's just Hoke the Hippo and his buddies taking a soak in a bunch of weeds."

"Let's get you to the shade, Guion," Rae sighed.
"The heat has gone to your head."

Not ready to give up, Guion hollered,
"Keep up, Rae! Let's try one more place!"

As Rae and Guion raced off,
Hoke grabbed a reed and tilted
his head, just like he had seen
Guion do. Hoke smiled widely
at the wonders he saw.

As the two friends entered the savannah,
Guion stopped quickly, squinted, and tilted his head.
"Now, don't be frightened, Rae. These are
friendly dinosaurs. They won't eat you ...
today!" he chuckled.

"Wow! Check out that T. rex!" shouted Guion.

Rae rubbed her eyes and looked around at the familiar landscape. Frustrated, she moaned, "What dinosaurs? All I see are some big trees and Olivia the Ostrich sitting on her nest."

Discouraged, Guion scratched his head and wandered off lost in thought.

Not wanting to disappoint her friend, Rae thought about the day. Why couldn't she see the castle or the mermaids? Then she remembered that Guion had squinted his eyes and tilted his head each time. She could give that a try.

Rae squinted her eyes and tilted her head. Was that a puff of smoke on top of the mountain? When she saw the terrifying T. rex, she knew for sure.

Jumping up and down, she exclaimed, "Holy smokes! I see it!" And it was the coolest thing she'd ever seen. Rae couldn't wait to tell Guion.

Rae found her friend sitting alone and asked,
"Hey Guion, what do you see now?"

He turned to her and responded,
"A pretty sunset. Right?"
Rae slowly shook her head and said, "No."

"It's not pretty, it's fantabulous!" Rae exclaimed. "Look at the giant Ferris wheel!"

"And the huge circus tents," Wilson the Giraffe added as she walked up behind them.

"I want to win one of those prizes!" Hoke the Hippo chimed in.

"And I can almost taste the cotton candy!" cried Olivia the Ostrich.

Guion looked around at his friends and a huge smile spread across his face.

"And the fireworks are incredible!" he shouted.

The friends leaned back to watch the final
colors fade into the dark savannah sky.

"I can't wait to see
what tomorrow will
bring," whispered Rae.

Guion hugged his friend and
nodded. "There is so much to see."

"Change the way you look at things,
and the things you look at change."

Dr. Wayne Dyer

The end.

LET'S TALK!

Questions about the Book

- What do you like about GUION'S character?

- What do you like about RAE'S character?

- What did you think when you saw GUION'S vision?
  How did it make you feel? What about it made you feel that way?

- What did you think when you saw RAE'S perspective of the scene?
  How did it make you feel? What about it made you feel that way?

- How do you think GUION felt when RAE couldn't see his vision?

- Have you experienced anything like this? How did it make you feel?

- When RAE was able to see the T. rex, how did that make you feel?

- When you look at the termite mound, the watering hole,
  or the savannah, what else might you see?

- Wilson the Giraffe and Hoke the Hippo were curious too.
  What did they see? Were you surprised at what they saw?

- Why do you think RAE kept trying to see what GUION was trying to show her?

- GUION sees the world from a creative point of view. Think of a place in your
  everyday world. What do you think GUION might see?

LET'S PLAY!

Activities for the Family

- **I SPY IN THE CLOUDS**: Clouds are full of fun shapes and images. Look up at the sky and use your imagination to transform clouds into pictures.

- **SCRIBBLE ADD-ON**: One person draws a scribble on a piece of paper. Each person in the group adds something to the scribble and passes it to the next person until a picture forms.

- **SCRIBBLE ART**: One person draws a scribble. Every person in the group traces the same scribble. Next, each individual makes their own drawing out of the scribble. Share your art with each other. How are things the same? How are the drawings different?

- **STORY ADD-ON**: One person begins the story by saying a few lines. The next person adds on to the story by saying "yes, and," then taking the plot wherever they want. Each person in the group takes at least one turn. The story is finished when the group says it is. If your group is large, you may want to set a time limit for each player.